13249

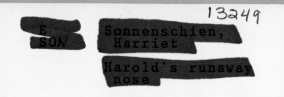

E
SON

Sonnenschien,
Harriet

Harold's runaway
nose

90-91 $12.95

DATE			
I-P			
JAN 24 91			
JAN 31 91			
FEB 7 91			
FEB 27 91			
MAR 7 91			
MAR 14 91			
APR 4 91			
APR 10 91			
APR 23 91			
JA 5 '95			

© THE BAKER & TAYLOR CO.

Harold's Runaway Nose

SIMON AND SCHUSTER BOOKS FOR YOUNG READERS
Simon & Schuster Building, Rockefeller Center, 1230 Avenue of the Americas,
New York, New York 10020
Copyright © 1989 by Harriet Sonnenschein. Illustrations © 1989 by Jürg Obrist.
SIMON AND SCHUSTER BOOKS FOR YOUNG READERS is a trademark of
Simon & Schuster Inc.
Manufactured in the United States of America
Typography by Mary Ahern.
10 9 8 7 6 5 4 3 2
Library of Congress Cataloging-in-Publication Data
Sonnenschein, Harriet.   Harold's runaway nose.
Summary: When Mrs. Rabbit tells her son Harold that his nose is running, he takes her
literally and chases his nose all over town.
[1. Rabbits—Fiction. 2. Nose—Fiction. 3. Humorous stories.]
I. Obrist, Jürg, ill.   II. Title.
PZ7.S699Har   1989   88-19797
ISBN 0-671-66912-5

Harold's Runaway Nose

by Harriet Sonnenschein · Illustrated by Jürg Obrist

Simon and Schuster Books For Young Readers

PUBLISHED BY SIMON & SCHUSTER INC., NEW YORK

For my daughters, Andrea, Ita and Racheli—HS

HAROLD used to look like an
ordinary bunny. He had soft fur,
long, fluffy ears, and a cute, little
pink nose—just like all the other
bunnies.

But one day that changed. Harold caught a cold. His fur was still soft. His ears were still long and fluffy. But his cute, little, pink nose turned into a big, red, stuffy nose. Harold was not happy.

Harold's mother brought him nose drops. "This will get rid of that big, red, stuffy nose," she told him. "Just tilt your head back."

She squeezed two drops into each nostril.

Harold wondered what was going to happen. He didn't want his nose to go away, just the cold. Would nose drops really make his nose drop off his face?

"You can lean forward now, Harold," his mother said.

Suddenly Harold felt frightened. He leaned his head forward very slowly. He could feel the stuffiness going away. Then he heard his mother calling, "For goodness' sake, Harold. Don't just stand there. Your nose is running!"

"Oh, no!" Harold panicked. "So my nose did drop off my face, just as I feared. And now it is running away. What shall I do!"

Quick as a flash, Harold was off and running, too. He was running after his runaway nose.

He ran through all the rooms in
his house. He searched up in the
attic.

He searched down in the cellar.

He searched out on the porch. But
he could not find his runaway nose.
There was only one other place
it could be. His nose must have run
into the garden.

"Harold, get your handkerchief," his mother told him.

"What a good idea," thought Harold. "I will use my handkerchief as a net. Then I will surely be able to catch my nose."

Harold raced into the garden with his handkerchief raised high in the air. He scurried across the grass and crawled through the bushes.

"Ah, ha!" he exclaimed, as he pulled out his nose from its hiding place under a thorny bush. But it wasn't his nose at all, just a plump, juicy raspberry.

"There it is, hiding among the flowers," Harold said. But when he got closer, Harold saw it was a lonely red rose—not his nose.

Harold hopped past all the bushes and shrubs. He got very tired. He wished that he could pause to catch his breath. But first he had to catch his nose!

Then Harold spotted it up in an oak tree, hiding in a pile of straw. He tried to trap it, but it flew away. "That isn't my nose, either," Harold realized. "It is a baby robin that I frightened away from its nest."

Harold grew very disappointed. He was sure he would never get his nose back. He had never felt so sad in his entire life. Harold began to cry. He cried and cried as he walked slowly back to his house.

When Harold's mother saw him, she asked, "What is the matter, Harold? Why are you crying?"

Harold tried to tell her that he wanted his nose back. But he was crying so hard that the words wouldn't come out. "I want…I want…I want…" was all that he could manage to sob.

Harold's mother became annoyed. "Oh, Harold, stop it! Just look at yourself. All that crying has brought your big, red, stuffy nose right back. Really, now, is that what you wanted?"

Harold ran to the mirror. Sure enough there was his big, red, stuffy nose right in the middle of his face, just where it belonged.

Harold stopped crying and jumped for joy. "Oh, yes, Mother," he answered excitedly. "That is exactly what I wanted!"